W9-DEY-768

HOW JOE THE BEAR AND SAM THE MOUSE GOT TOGETHER

With many thanks to Tamara Kitt and to Bernice and to Dorothy and to Cindy.

 Inquiries should be addressed to Lothrop, Lee & Shepard Books, a division of William Morrow & Company, Inc., 105 Madison Avenue, New York, New York 10016. Printed in Singapore.

First Edition 1 2 3 4 5 6 7 8 9 10

Library of Congress Cataloging in Publication Data
De Regniers, Beatrice Schenk. How Joe the bear and Sam the mouse got together / by Beatrice Schenk de Regniers; illustrated by Bernice Myers.
p. cm. Summary: The friendship of Joe the Bear and Sam the Mouse blossoms when they find something they both like to do. ISBN 0-688-09079-6.—ISBN 0-688-09080-X (lib. bdg.) [1. Bears—Fiction. 2. Mice—Fiction. 3. Friendship—Fiction.] I. Myers, Bernice, ill. II. Title. PZ7.D4417Ho 1990 [E]—dc20
89-12110 CIP AC

BEATRICE SCHENK DE REGNIERS

HOW JOE THE BEAR AND SAM THE MOUSE GOT TOGETHER

ILLUSTRATED BY
BERNICE MYERS

LOTHROP, LEE & SHEPARD BOOKS
NEW YORK

Call me Joe.
Call me Sam.

Hi, Sam. **Hi, Joe.**

Where are you going,
Sam?
Where are YOU going,
Joe?

I am looking
for a place to live.
I am looking
for a place to live, too.
We can live together!

I like to live
in a BIG house.
I like to live
in a little house.

Then we cannot live together.

Boo hoo.

Boo hoo.

Do you like
to play ball?
Yes.
I love to play ball.

We can play ball together!
I like to play football.
I like to
play baseball.

Then we cannot
play ball together.

Boo hoo!

Do you like to ride a bike?

**Yes.
I love to ride a bike.**

We can ride a bike together!
I like to ride slow.
I like to ride fast.

Then we cannot
ride a bike together.

Boo hoo.

Boo hoo.

Do you like music?
Yes.
I love music.

We can play music together!
I like violin music.
I like drum music.

I hate drum music.

I hate violin music.

Then we cannot play music together.
Boo hoo.
Good-bye, Sam.
Boo hoo.
Good-bye, Joe.

Where are you going,
Sam?
Where are YOU going,
Joe?

It is three o'clock.
I am going to get ice cream.
Every day at three o'clock
I eat ice cream.

What kind
of ice cream
do you eat,
Sam?

All kinds of ice cream.

I eat all kinds
of ice cream,
too.

Then we can eat ice cream together!

You will live in a big house.
I will live in a little house.

You will play football and ride slow.
I will play baseball and ride fast.

You will play violin music.
I will play drum music.

But every day
at three o'clock...

Yes. Every day
at three o'clock...

...we will eat ice cream together!